D0347524

This book belongs to

....

Peppa Pig™

LADYBIRD BOOKS
UK | USA | Canada | Ireland | Australia | India | New Zealand | South Africa

Ladybird Books is part of the Penguin Random House group of companies
whose addresses can be found at global.penguinrandomhouse.com.

www.penguin.co.uk www.puffin.co.uk www.ladybird.co.uk

Penguin Random House UK

First published 2022
001

Adapted by Toria Hegedus

Printed in China

The authorized representative in the EEA is Penguin Random House Ireland,
Morrison Chambers, 32 Nassau Street, Dublin D02 YH68

A CIP catalogue record for this book is available from the British Library

ISBN: 978-0-241-54338-2

All correspondence to:
Ladybird Books, Penguin Random House Children's
One Embassy Gardens, 8 Viaduct Gardens, London SW11 7BW

FSC® www.fsc.org
MIX
Paper from responsible sources
FSC® C018179

Granny and Grandpa Pig's Day Out

It was a lovely sunny day. Peppa and George were at
Granny and Grandpa Pig's house, helping Grandpa Pig
with his raspberry patch.

Suddenly, a little bird swooped down and stole a raspberry.

"Hee! Hee! The little birds like your raspberries, Grandpa,"
said Peppa.
"So do I!" huffed Grandpa Pig. "Good job I'm here to make
sure those pesky birds don't eat them all."

Just then, Granny Pig came outside. "I've had a wonderful idea," she said. "Let's go camping!"
"Oooh!" said Peppa and George.
"Good thinking, Granny Pig," said Grandpa Pig. "We can camp in the garden. I can keep my eyes on my raspberries that way!"

"Actually, I thought we'd go to the beach," said Granny Pig.
"We love the beach!" cheered Peppa.
"And that's not the best part . . ." said Granny Pig mysteriously.

Granny Pig led everyone to the shed. "I thought it'd be fun to take *this* for the trip," she said, pulling off an old sheet.

"It's a shiny red motorbike!" said Peppa. "But what's the funny thing on the side?"
"It's called a *sidecar*, Peppa," said Granny Pig. "You and George can sit in it."

"Grandpa Pig and I went on lots of motorbiking adventures when we were younger," said Granny Pig. "We camped on mountains, in the jungle and even on an iceberg!"

"Oooh!" cried Peppa. "This is going
to be so much fun!"

Soon, everyone was packed and ready to set off.
"It is very important to be safe when you're on a motorbike,"
said Granny Pig. "You must **always** wear a helmet!"
"I'm wearing a helmet *and* goggles," said Peppa.

Granny Pig started the engine. *BRMMMMM! BRMMMMM!*
"It's VERY loud!" shouted Peppa. She began to sing.

"Granny's motorbike goes
BRRM, BRRM, BRRM!
All day long . . ."

When they arrived at the beach, Granny Pig said, "This looks like the perfect spot to camp!" She pressed a button and – *boing!* – a tent popped out from the motorbike.

"A magic tent!" cried Peppa. "Amazing!"
"Yes, Peppa," said Grandpa Pig, chuckling.
"The motorbike has everything we need . . ."

Boing!

"... even my raspberries!" finished Grandpa Pig. He opened a special flap on the tent. "I'd like to see those pesky birds get at them now."

Suddenly . . . *Squawk!*
Oh dear. A cheeky seagull had spotted
Grandpa Pig's raspberries!
"Er, perhaps it's time to explore the shore,
children," said Granny Pig.

Squawk!

Squawk!

When they reached the shore, Peppa and Granny Pig played in the water. Suddenly, Peppa spotted something on the sand.

"What's that?" said Peppa.
George lifted up a piece of rope. "Trea-sure!"
"Sometimes things that were in the ocean
wash up on the beach," explained Granny Pig.
"Sea treasure!" cried Peppa.

Peppa and George searched
for more sea treasure.
"Look, Granny!" said Peppa,
showing off some shiny shells.
"How wonderful," said
Granny Pig, smiling.

But, when another wave came in, more things washed up –
and those things were not treasure. They were rubbish!
"A plastic bottle," gasped Peppa. "And another . . . and another!"
"They must have been in the sea," said Granny Pig sadly. "They
don't belong there."
"Let's clean them up!" said Peppa.

Peppa and George picked up *lots* of bottles.

"Oh!" said Peppa. "This one has **something inside!**"

"It looks like a message," said Granny Pig, opening it.

"Hello, my name is Little Reggie Rabbit. I am on holiday with my mummy and daddy!" she read.

"There's a telephone number," cried Peppa.
"Can we ring it? *Pleeease?*"
Granny Pig dialled the number and passed her
phone to Peppa.

Ring!
Ring!

"Hello," said a voice on the other end of the phone. "Grampy Rabbit speaking!"
"Can we talk to Little Reggie Rabbit, please?" said Peppa.

"There isn't a *little* Reggie Rabbit here," replied Grampy Rabbit, "but there is a *big* Reggie Rabbit!"

"Oh," sighed Peppa. "We found a message in a bottle from Little Reggie Rabbit."

"That was my message, Peppa," said Grampy Rabbit. "I threw it into the sea when I was very small!"

"You must not throw things into the sea, Grampy Rabbit!" Peppa gasped.
"I know that now," said Grampy Rabbit. "There is too much rubbish in the ocean. Thank you for cleaning it up!"

"That's OK," said Peppa. "We found lots of sea treasures, too!"
"Sea treasures, *hmm*?" said Grampy Rabbit. "Perhaps you can make something from what you've picked up. I love recycling old junk into useful things!"

After the phone call ended, Peppa, George and Granny Pig went back to the tent to see Grandpa Pig.
"These cheeky seagulls won't leave my poor raspberries alone," he said. "If only I had something to shoo them away with . . ."

shoo!

"I know!" said Peppa.
"We can use our sea treasures
to make something to keep
the birds away!"

Peppa, George, Granny and Grandpa Pig began to build a bird-scarer. They used Peppa's shells, George's rope and all the old bottles they had picked up on the beach.

Soon, the bird-scarer was complete.

"The wind shakes the shells and bottles" explained Peppa, "and the noise of them hitting together shoos the birds!"

Squawk!

Rattle! Rattle!

"My raspberries are safe at last!" cheered Grandpa Pig. "Thank you, Peppa and George!"

The next morning, it was time to go home. Grandpa Pig
packed his raspberry patch . . . and the bird-scarer, too.
"Next time we go camping, you'll have to find more
sea treasures," he told Peppa and George. "Then my
whole garden will be safe!"
Everyone laughed. "Hee! Hee! Hee!"

Peppa loves sea treasures.
Everyone loves sea treasures!